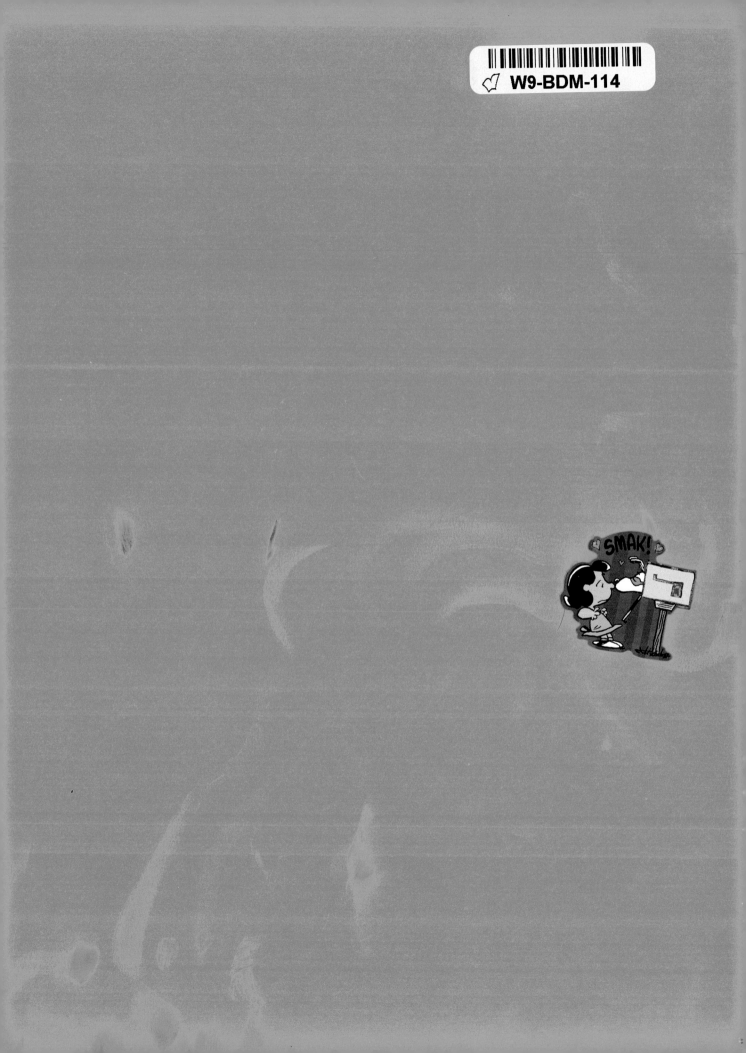

POCO LOCO

By **J. R. Krause** and **Maria Chua**

Amazon Children's Publishing

For Catherine and Sonja

J. R. Krause and **Maria Chua** are a husband and wife team living in Southern California. Maria attended the University of Madrid, Spain, and lived in Mexico. She is a bilingual psychiatric social worker in Los Angeles. J. R. is an artist, designer, and animator working in television. Currently he is a designer for *The Simpsons*. This is their first picture book. To learn more visit: www.jrkrause.com

Text and illustrations copyright © 2013 by J. R. Krause and Maria Chua

Amazon Publishing
Attn: Amazon Children's Publishing
P.O. Box 400818
Las Vegas, NV 89140
www.amazon.com/amazonchildrenspublishing

ISBN-13: 9781477816493 (hardcover)
ISBN-10: 1477816496 (hardcover)
ISBN-13: 9781477866498 (eBook)
ISBN-10: 1477866493 (eBook)

The illustrations are rendered in digital media.

Book design by Vera Soki
Editor: Marilyn Brigham

Printed in China (R)
First edition
10 9 8 7 6 5 4 3 2 1

GLOSSARY OF SPANISH WORDS

alto (AHL-toe): stop

arándanos (ah-RAHN-dah-nos): blueberries

arriba (ah-REE-bah): up

azúcar (a-SU-kar): sugar

buen provecho (boo-en pro-VAY-cho): enjoy your meal

café (cah-fay): coffee

cerdo (SER-do): pig

crema (KRAY-mah): cream

delicioso (day-lee-cee-OH-so): delicious

fresas (FRAY-sahs): strawberries

gallo (GA-yo): rooster

gato (GAH-toe): cat

genio (HAY-nee-o): genius

helicóptero (ay-lee-COP-tay-roh): helicopter

lluvia (YOO-vee-ah): rain

loco (LO-ko): crazy

mal tiempo (mahl tee-EM-po): bad weather

masa (mah-sah): batter

máxima (MAHC-see-mah): maximum

mi (mee): my

paraguas (pah-RAH-gwas): umbrella

poco (PO-ko): little

ratón (rah-TONE): mouse

vaca (VAH-cah): cow

wafle (ua-fel): waffle

POCO LOCO is a very unusual *ratón*.
He invents wacky things.

Take for example the "Cuckoo
Clock–Coffeemaker." It's heavy on
the cuckoo!
  And the Shower-Bed—most
think it's just plain *loco*. That's
why everyone calls him Poco Loco.

Today Poco Loco is using the Waffle Iron–Weather Forecaster. It makes hot, fluffy waffles and predicts the weather.
"My machine is predicting *mal tiempo*—oh no! I have to warn my friends!"

"Hey! Let's eat breakfast in the barn!" squeaks Poco Loco.

"Inside? On such a beautiful day?" crows Gallo.

"No way! The picnic parade has already begun," meows Gato.

"Ay, Poco Loco," oinks Cerdo.

"He's one crazy mouse," moos Vaca. "We're eating outside today."

"But *mal tiempo* is coming!" squeaks Poco Loco. "Quick! Get under my trusty *paraguas*!"

MAL TIEMPO

Suddenly a roar of wind whips through the picnic.
Poco Loco's trusty *paraguas* flips up, up, and away.

ALTO

"¡Ay, Poco Loco!"

Gallo runs!
Gallo jumps!
Gallo grabs tight—

. . . and Gallo takes flight!

MAL TiEMPO

Gato runs!
Gato jumps!
Gato grips tight—

. . . and Gato takes flight!

"¡AY, POCO LOCO!"

Cerdo runs!
Cerdo jumps!
Cerdo holds on tight—

. . . and Cerdo takes flight!

Vaca runs!
Vaca jumps!
Vaca clasps tight—

. . . and Vaca takes flight!

"¡AY, NO! ¡LLUVIA!"

Vaca slips.
Cerdo slips.
Gato slips.
Gallo slips . . .

ALTO

"MOO!"

"COCK-A
DOODLE
DOO!"

Suddenly Poco Loco remembers what
is perhaps his greatest invention of all.
He squeaks, "Never fear . . .

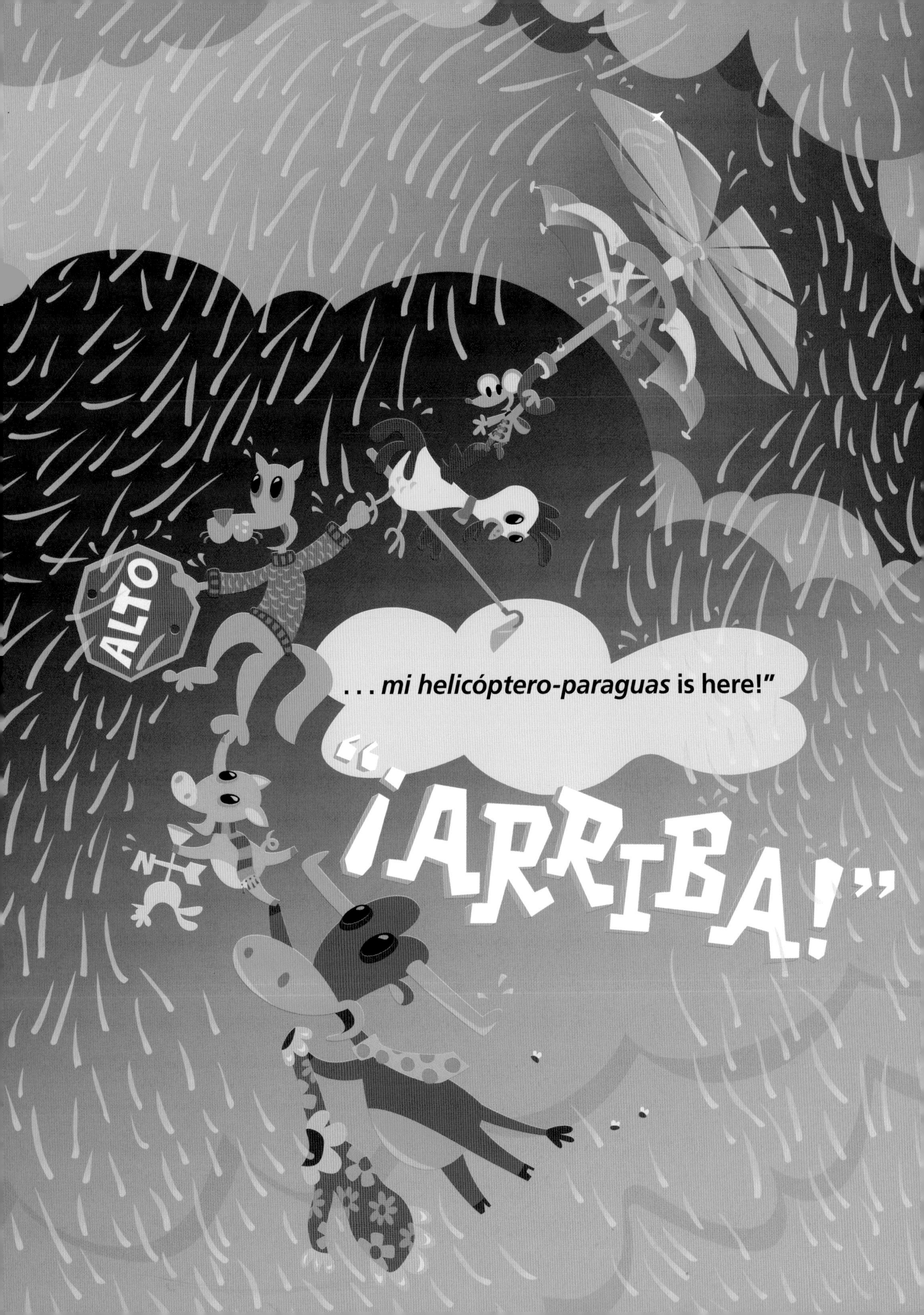

. . . *mi helicóptero-paraguas* is here!"

"¡ARRIBA!"

Gallo, Gato, Cerdo, and Vaca cheer—

"¡AY, POCO...

DRATS! Breakfast is GONE WITH THE WIND!

ALTO

You must admit, Poco Loco is a very unusual *ratón*.